Also by
Joy Ross Davis

Beggar's Miracle

Countenance

Mother, Can You Hear Me?

The Transformation of Bitty Brown

Be not forgetful to entertain strangers:

for thereby some have entertained angels unaware.

Hebrews 13: 2

Emalyn's
TREASURE

Joy Ross Davis

Windswept

Livonia, Michigan

Emalyn's Treasure

Published by Windswept
an imprint of BHC Press

Library of Congress Control Number:
2017933760

ISBN-13: 978-1-946006-63-9
ISBN-10: 1-946006-63-7

Visit the author at:
www.joyrossdavis.com &
www.bhcpress.com

Also available in eBook

Book design by Blue Harvest Creative
www.blueharvestcreative.com

With grateful acknowledgment
to Murray Pura,
an institution all his own.

For Kristiaan

Rest in the arms of angels

1

The Tragedy

The Lady Emalyn kept her treasure in a cobalt blue box sewn into the cushion of her green velvet chair. She had hidden it there when she was six, and in the fifteen years since, her treasure had remained untouched and unseen by another living soul.

On the rare occasion when she was alone at night, when her husband Owen traveled to the next town on business, she often whispered, "No, it wouldn't do. I can't tell him. I can't tell anyone."

Each morning she ran her hand over the velvet chair. Her treasure, safe inside, caused a slight stiffness in one corner of the cushion. When her family had moved from Dungarran to London in 1926, Emalyn cried until her father agreed to bring along the odd velvet chair, its scalloped back and generous width quite cumbersome. At only eight, the girl—the only child—could bend her father's will to her own with a tear or two.

In 1931, her family moved again, the call of their beloved Ireland simply too strong to resist. When they returned, the green chair had journeyed with them and taken its place in Emalyn's bedroom in her father's house—Dunaghy Manor—a grand three-story befitting the Earl of Dungarran and his family, a home for which they all felt a special reverence.

That they were a family blessed by God no one would argue. A personable, wealthy landowner father; a beautiful, gentle and gracious mother; and their only child, the stunning little red-haired beauty named Emalyn, Lady Emalyn to the residents of Dungarran. They had known little sorrow or trouble, and except for the incident involving Emalyn when she was six, their lives had not been touched by tragedy. Their home was a peaceable kingdom abounding in a love that encouraged the very best in all of them, from the father's almost golden business acumen to the mother's magic touch in the home and surrounding gardens, and even to Emalyn whose talents flourished as she grew. An extraordinary chocolatier, the stunning beauty bore no detectable effects of the early tragedy, though everyone in town thought she certainly should.

It was, after all, an encounter that almost took her life.

In 1934, long after Emalyn's encounter, the family suffered its first—and most horrific—tragedy. Both father and mother attended a social event, a celebration of the completed construction of Dungarran's own High Cross. The original had been built in the 1600s and had fallen into ruin. But on this day in 1934, the Earl of Dungarran, along with his lifelong friend Thomas Meade, the cheese maker, both members of the county's Electric and Water Supply Board, awaited the unveiling of the cross. It would serve as a testament to the growth of Dungarran from a dying village to a thriving township, the seat of the county's council. The two men, both wealthy in their own right... in part because of their use of electricity and water...commissioned the Celtic, ornately-carved stone cross to be built and placed at the entrance to the town.

It was, perhaps, one of their proudest days.

The Lady Emalyn, boxed chocolates in hand and running a little late, hurried along the road toward the celebration, stumbling occasionally on clods of dirt or errant stones caught in the heels of her pumps. Owen Meade, her fiancé, walked happily beside her, often bending to whisper in her ear and see her smile, or lending a hand when she tripped. The quarter-mile walk, which they'd done together many times to deliver cheese and chocolates as gifts to ailing friends, took longer than usual, and by the time they were almost there, a bright light flashed ahead, one neither had never seen before.

Emalyn and Owen stopped.

The light pulsed for a moment then went out, followed almost instantly by an explosion that knocked them both to the ground, and when they got to their feet, they felt both shock and an almost overwhelming grief. Not only had the Dunaghy-Meade High Cross been destroyed, but the two of them, at nineteen, were now orphans.

A year later, they were husband and wife and clung to their love for each other as if it might disappear at any moment. The two of them lived in Dunaghy Manor as the Meade house had been partially destroyed by a second, but less powerful, bomb. That Dunaghy Manor still stood unharmed seemed a miracle to them both.

Living with them in the Dunaghy house were Fiona and her son, Percy. Fiona had been with the family since shortly after Father and Mother had married. Her own husband had died and left her penniless and starving, so she appealed for help to her dear friend who was now married to the Earl of Dungarran. Immediately, Fiona was employed as housekeeper and never spent another day wracked by cold or hunger.

When Emalyn was born, Fiona found new purpose in her life. As yet childless, Fiona looked upon sweet Emalyn as the daughter she didn't have and devoted most of her skills and time to making sure the child felt loved, even adored, a feeling that Fiona herself had never known.

Emalyn thrived under Fiona's care, and then Percy entered their lives.

He changed everything.

2

The Garden

The Lady Emalyn contained her excitement by puttering in the garden and gathering mint for a new recipe in her chocolate making. A rain storm earlier in the day gave the short sprigs a wonderful aroma that she thought might be well received by the many friends who loved her little chocolate candies.

She gathered a handful of mint, sniffed it, and smiled.

"Ah, yes," she whispered, "I shall make some for tonight's celebration."

"And who might you be talking to?" Fiona asked.

"Myself, I guess," Emalyn said and laughed. "It's such a grand day, isn't it?"

"Aye, 'tis that, my girl," Fiona said and brushed a stray lock of hair from the girl's face. "And you'll be lovely, the loveliest one at the party. Imagine that you've been married three years already."

"The time has flown so quickly that I can hardly believe it. Oh, here," she said and held the sprigs toward Fiona's face, "smell this."

"Mint, yes, it's heavenly, but we really don't need it for tonight's feast. I have plenty already."

"I'm trying a new recipe for my chocolates," she said. "Fiona?"

"Yes, dear?"

"I've been thinking about something." Emalyn fiddled with the handful of mint. "Maybe one day, I could…I might have a little chocolate shop. Is that ridiculous?"

Fiona smiled.

"I think it's brilliant," Fiona said. "Just brilliant."

Just then, Emalyn heard footsteps along the garden pathway. A loud, melodious male voice called, "Is it my swan I hear?"

A smile came across Emalyn's face, and she called back, "'Tis your swan, my love."

Owen stepped from behind the corner of the house. Tall, broad-shouldered, and fair-haired, he wore a white collared shirt, baggy tan trousers, a dark sweater vest, and two-tone Oxfords. The boxing champion for years at their school, he had powerfully muscular arms that never failed to strain the sleeves of his shirts.

"Just look at my handsome husband. You look as if you've just stepped out of the pages of a magazine."

"Ah, my swan," he said and hugged his petite wife tightly to him.

Fiona waved at him and went back into the kitchen.

"I'm afraid I look more like an ugly duckling than a swan today," Emalyn said and smiled up at him. "I've been working in the garden. Just look at my Wellies covered in mud."

"No, but no. It would take more than a little mud to lessen your stunning beauty."

He picked her up in his arms and spun around, the sound of their laughter ringing throughout the many gardens.

"I am the luckiest man on earth," he whispered to her, kissing her softly. "And have I told you that swans mate for life? If their partner dies, they could pass away from a broken heart."

"Yes, my darling, you've told me many times. But nothing will happen to us. We will be together forever," Emalyn said and kissed him hard on the lips. "Happy Anniversary, my dearest."

Owen set her gently on the ground and looked at her quizzically.

"Anniversary?" he said. "Is that today?"

Owen clasped his hands behind his back and turned away from her. Then he turned back quickly.

"You're sure it's today? I thought it was next Tuesday. Hmmm," he said and walked away again. He disappeared behind the side of the house.

Emalyn narrowed her eyes.

Now, what is he up to this time?

"Emalyn, dear, can you come 'round here for a moment?" Fiona called to her from the side of the house.

"Fiona, I thought you were in the kitchen. Is something wrong with Owen? I can't believe it," she said, shaking her heard. "That man's forgotten our anniversary again!"

Emalyn stopped as soon as she saw Owen and Fiona standing together.

"Happy Anniversary, my little swan," Owen said and beamed.

He and Fiona held a beautiful white satin formal gown, with a coral and green floral chiffon overlay on the skirt. Yellow, white, and coral roses lined the neck of the gown with matching ones forming a bouquet at the waist in the back. The gorgeous chiffon draped out into a long train.

Emalyn gasped and put her hands over her mouth.

Owen's smile faded.

"What's wrong? Don't you like it? I...I thought you'd...I thought..."

His wife moved her hands away from her mouth.

15

"I adore it," she said as tears slid down her face. "Oh, Owen, it's one of the loveliest gowns I've ever seen."

Owen handed the dress to Fiona and hugged Emalyn so tightly she could barely breathe.

"I'm so relieved. For a moment, I thought you hated it."

Emalyn stood back, cocked her head to the side, and grinned up at him.

"Well, you did say you'd forgotten," she said and batted her eyelashes.

Owen laughed out loud.

"I'm taking the dress in now before it gets filthy," Fiona said. "Mind you, come along so we can get you ready for your big night."

"Mammy!" someone called. "Mammy!"

The three of them turned to see a boy of about twelve walking toward them. Short and stocky, he walked with a pronounced limp. He wore a cap, the bill pulled down low and a nice woolen coat. Blood oozed from his nose, and his right eye was bruised and swollen.

"Mercy," Fiona scolded. "What have you been into now? Are you all right, boy?"

"I'll take the dress," Emalyn said and reached out to Fiona. "You tend to Percy."

"Got a bitta mud on yer boots, eh?" Percy said. "Imagine the Lady Emalyn with mud on her boots. Wonder what she'd look like with blood on her pretty little skirt?"

"Hush your mouth, Percy, and get in this house so I can tend to ya," Fiona said.

Percy lunged as if he were coming near Emalyn, but Owen stepped in front of her.

"Go on in the house now," Owen said, "and let your mammy look after you."

Percy balled his fists and swiped at the air close to Owen's face.

In one smooth move, Owen swept Emalyn behind his back and moved them both to the side and out of harm's way. At more than a foot taller than the short but stocky boy, Owen had little trouble.

Fiona was behind the boy in a split second, her fingers pinching one of his ears.

"Go on with ya, now. Hear me? You act like an animal when these folks have treated you like family all these years."

"Ow," Percy yelled.

But Fiona held onto that ear as she dragged the yowling boy into the house.

"It's the strap for you, hear me?" she said as they disappeared inside.

Emalyn, the beautiful dress in her arms, sat in the white wicker rocking chair and folded the dress carefully so that it would not touch the ground. Owen slipped in beside her and put his arm around her narrow shoulders.

"You're trembling," he said. "Don't be worried, love. The boy's a rounder, for sure, but I think he's harmless."

"He struck at you, Owen! Percy's not harmless. He's always been this way, always looking for trouble, always into scrapes, always sneaking around in the house getting into things. Why, once, years ago, I even found him in my room!"

"And what was he doing in there? Did he pull all your clothes from the wardrobe? Scatter everything about?"

Emalyn frowned.

"Worse," she said. "Much worse."

"Tell me, then. What was he doing?"

"He was in my chair, Owen, my velvet chair, sitting there running his hands over the cushion."

"And what age would he have been, then?"

"Seven, I think. I can't remember exactly."

Owen got up and pulled Emalyn to her feet.

"Worry yourself not, my swan. Percy came to you suffering, and though his body has partially healed, his mind and soul are struggling. Something about that boy touches my heart."

Emalyn shook her head.

"I just don't trust him. He's just a boy, but he....he frightens me. I can't explain why."

Owen opened the kitchen door for her then kissed her hard on her full lips.

"All the more reason to be tolerant," he said and kissed her again. "My beautiful swan. Go now, and put on that lovely dress. Our grand celebration is only a few hours away."

Owen bent and picked up a bundle off the ground.

"Your mint," he said and handed it to her. "For the special chocolates."

"Thank you, my dear. I must have dropped it."

Owen tucked a strand of hair behind Emalyn's ear. "Some special confection for our anniversary?

"You'll see," Emalyn said and winked at him.

Owen cupped her face in his hands and lifted it gently. "You are the light of my life, the joy of my being."

"Tell me," she said. "Tell me again."

Owen chuckled and kissed the top of her head.

"I am the sun," he whispered close to her ear. "And you, the moon. Our love is like them both, for the sun loved the moon so much that he died every night just to let her breathe."

The Foundling

E malyn crushed the mint for her candies with a mortar and pestle made of expensive Connemara marble, a gift from her mother and father when she was only eight years old.

As the rich dark chocolate simmered on the stove, she sprinkled the fine particles into the mixture and added a touch of brandy. She watched carefully to gauge the consistency and thickness. The sweet aroma filled the downstairs. She removed the mixture from the heat and stirred until it began to temper. Then, with a steady and skilled hand, she poured it into her special molds. She'd chosen her favorites, the ones she had ordered from France, those with small images of a high cross stamped onto the bottom. When she'd filled all three molds, she topped each candy with a tiny white chocolate swan.

"They'll be wonderful," she said and wiped her hands on her apron. She glanced at the fine particles of mint swirled into the bittersweet chocolate and the swan atop each one. "Perfect. My Owen will love them."

Tenderly, she moved the molds to the bottom slot of the new Shelvadore refrigerator that Owen had purchased for them only a year ago. Emalyn was especially fond of this new treasure in her kitchen since the door had cooling shelves and there was ample room on the interior shelves, as well. It made her work and Fiona's so much easier and more efficient.

"The candies smell wonderful," Fiona said as she walked into the kitchen. "Wonderful!"

Emalyn smiled. "The mint and brandy will work well together, I think."

"Did you use the high cross molds? And the little swan on top?"

Emalyn giggled. "You know me too well, Fiona. I hope Owen will be pleased."

"He'd be pleased with anything your lovely hands made, my girl."

Emalyn wiped her hands again on her apron and tossed a dirty hand towel into the clothes basket in the nook beside the kitchen. Then she untied her apron and dropped it in the basket, too. Without looking at Fiona, she asked about Percy.

"Oh, that boy," Fiona said and dropped into a chair. "Sometimes, I think..." her voice trailed off.

"He'll be all right," Emalyn said, still without letting her eyes meet Fiona's. "You've treated him with such loving care. How could he not be all right?"

"But he cut my time short with you, my girl. He ruined so many things. I know that, and I hope you'll forgive me if I ever neglected you on account of him, but he....he was just so needy then, as he still is now. Every day, it seems, there's some new trouble about him. I've tried," she said as tears rolled down her face, "but I feel a sense of failure."

Emalyn knelt beside her.

"No, you've not failed either of us, Fiona. You're only one person. You take care of me and this house and still, you find time for mothering Percy. You've done your best."

Fiona buried her face in the skirt of her apron and wept.

Emalyn stood and wrung her hands. Then she went to the sink and wet a hand towel. It was all she could think of to do.

"Here now," she said in a soft, soothing voice. "Wipe those tears away. You've been the best mother anyone could ask for, a blessing to Percy. When no one else wanted him, you took him in and then adopted him. You've given him the very best, Fiona."

Fiona wiped her eyes and sat up straight.

"He's up to something, my girl. I know it in my mother's heart. Those ruffians he runs with are no good, their dads neither, all of 'em opposed our own good Mr. Dunaghy and Mr. Meade." Fiona crossed herself. "God rest their souls. And now, they're talking against your Owen. I'm afraid of their influence on Percy. Aye, he's all bluster and brag, but inside, he's still a frightened little boy with a limp that causes him pain and ridicule. The poor boy has known such pain."

Emalyn nodded. "I remember."

Emalyn thought back to the day they found him, just a baby, right there on their doorstep outside the kitchen. He was screaming and wailing, wearing nothing but a diaper in the freezing cold, tears and mucous caked all over his little face. His eyes were crusted shut. And one of his legs was so badly broken that it shot out at an odd angle. The baby looked as if he'd been beaten over every inch of his small body.

"He claimed my heart on the day we found him," Fiona said, "and hasn't let go of it since. Day after day, night after night, we sat with him and held him. Your father had the best doctors to set his little leg. We fed him 'til he could eat no more, and that boy has not known hunger or cold since. Praise the sweet Lord for that."

"And we've never been able to find out about his real parents," Emalyn said, "even with all of Papa's efforts with detectives and the *garda*, the police."

Fiona shook her head.

"We've never had an inkling," she said. "I used to tell Percy, when he'd ask me how his leg got hurt, that he was a wee angel who toppled down from Heaven and landed on some rough stone. He'd always ask, 'If I was an angel, Mam, why didn't God protect me?' And I'd answer, 'Well, now, He did, didn't He. Our Father in Heaven sent you straight from your fall to the steps of Dunaghy Manor and into my waiting arms.'"

Emalyn patted Fiona's hands.

"No one could have loved him more than you," she said.

"'Tis true, I think," Fiona said. "Well, we've no more time for this. There's a feast to ready for tonight's celebration. Will ya hand me a clean apron, my girl, the one with the rose on it? But I'll go and fetch Percy first to let him eat before any of the guests come. Lord only knows how he'd act given the state he's been in today."

"Shall I have Owen do that, Fiona? He has a heart for the boy."

"Have Owen do what?"

Emalyn turned to see Owen standing in the doorway. Dressed in his finest cuffed linen pants, white collared shirt, silk tie, and tweed vest, he was the handsomest man she'd ever seen. His blond hair, short in the back but longer in the front so that it occasionally fell across his forehead and his finely chiseled nose and cheekbones gave him the look of an ancient god.

He smiled at her and bowed low, gesturing with his large hands.

"Your wish is my command, my swan."

"Lordy me, I've never seen such," Fiona said. "You'd think you two were wed just yesterday."

Emalyn felt a blush rising in her cheeks.

"Blushing like a new bride," Owen said and hugged her. "And what is it you desire of me?"

"Would you be a dear," Emalyn said and ran her small hand down Owen's tanned cheek, "and fetch Percy for us? Fiona wants him to be fed and off to bed before any of our guests arrive. And I must go upstairs and get ready myself."

For a few seconds, she felt herself caught by Owen's beautiful blue eyes, caught and held as if in a trance. The scent of his cologne, a new French one called Caron, wafted its exotic but subtle floral notes around her. Arrested by his presence, Emalyn gazed into those eyes.

Owen took her face in her hands and whispered, "I am the sun."

"And I am the moon," Emalyn said.

"And I will die each night just to let you breathe."

Fiona sniffed and brushed a tear from her eye.

When Owen had kissed his wife softly on the cheek, he turned. "I'm off," he said, "to fetch Master Percy."

"And I am off to make myself beautiful for our festivities."

"Then it shouldn't take very long," Owen said as he left.

Before Emalyn left the kitchen, she checked her cooling chocolates, made sure each white swan sat securely atop its chocolate companion, and tested with her finger to make certain of the texture.

"Perfect," she said to Fiona.

Owen and Percy came in just as she was leaving to go upstairs. Emalyn was shocked to see how badly swollen the boy's eye and nose had become. In spite of her slight fear of him, her sense of justice prevailed. She could not leave without trying to find out who had done this to him, so she sat across from him at the small table.

"Will you tell us who hurt you, Percy?"

Fiona set a plate of steaming roast pork and vegetables and a heaping mound of potatoes in front of him. He dove into it greedily.

Owen stood beside the boy and put a hand on his shoulder.

"Percy, did you have lunch today?"

Percy nodded his head.

"And what would that have been, then lad? What sort of lunch did your Mam prepare for you?

23

Emalyn saw Owen glance at Fiona, who'd stopped her vegetable chopping to look at him.

Percy shrugged.

"Same as always," he said without looking up from his plate.

Fiona slid her arm across the boy's shoulders.

"So, what did you think of the special treat I put in the bag for you?"

"A treat, now what would that have been I wonder?" Owen said. "You're a lucky boy to get a treat in your lunch sack."

"Oh, tell us, Percy. What was it?" Emalyn asked. "What special treat did your mam give you?"

Percy shoveled the last bits of food into his mouth.

"I'm finished now, Mam. I'm not feeling well. May I go back to bed?"

"Well, look at you using your manners," Owen said.

Fiona smiled at the boy. "You may certainly go back to bed, love, just as soon as you tell us about the special treat in your sack."

Percy lowered his head and mumbled, "Chocolates, the ones made by Miss Emalyn."

"Run along to be now, Percy. Your mam will check on you shortly," Owen said. "And I'll pop in before the celebration begins."

Emalyn watched Owen as he peeped around the door when Percy left.

Then, he turned to her and Fiona.

"Well, did you put chocolates in his lunch?"

Fiona shook her head.

"I put an extra biscuit with some sausages. They're his favorites. And one of those sweet oranges you brought us from the market. But why would he lie about it?"

"He didn't lie," Owen said and rubbed his forehead. "The boy didn't lie because he didn't know what was in the bag."

"But how could he not know what was in his own lunch bag?" Emalyn asked.

24

"It's just as I've suspected for a good while, why he's so hungry every evening, eating as if he were half starved. Those hooligans he's hanging out with are stealing his lunch. They probably get it first thing every morning."

"Then we should go right to the school and report it. We know Principal O'Hara and his whole family. He would help."

"I've no proof, Emmy, and Percy won't tell for fear of what they'd do. They already tease and batter him about his limp. Principal O'Hara is a good man, but he's no match for that group of ruffians."

"There must be something we can do," Emalyn said. "Surely we can think of some way to stop them. We have to help him, Owen."

Owen was about to speak when the doorbell rang.

Emalyn gasped.

"Oh, mercy! Look at the time! I'll be late for my own anniversary party."

4

Treasures

Emalyn slipped out of her dirty clothes, washed herself off, and stepped into the beautiful dress that Owen had given her. She straightened the ruffled straps on her shoulders, adjusted the row of pink and yellow roses lining the neck then turned to do the same with the large roses that graced the waist of the low-cut back. She fumbled with the hooks, finally secured them, then fluffed out the floral overlay. The chiffon trailed out behind her for three or four feet.

She gazed at herself in the mirror.

My hair. Oh, my hair.

At the vanity, she brushed out her hair, pulled it tightly back from her face and twisted the thick red mass into a chignon, her nimble fingers working to secure it with a multitude of pins. When it was tight and smooth, she slid in the large jeweled comb, turned her head, and smiled. Rouge, lipstick, and a bit of mascara completed the look.

At the shoe closet, she surveyed her choices and settled on the green satin heels, the very same color as the floral leaves in the chiffon.

Instinctively, she walked to the velvet chair, felt the cushion, smiled when her fingers lingered at the small stiffened section and whispered a prayer of thanks for her treasure and for the many blessings in her life. Her prayer of thanks turned into a plea for the safety of Percy.

When he'd come into their lives twelve years ago, a pitiful, abandoned, and sickly orphan, Emalyn had tried to love him, but Percy required round-the-clock care. Her mother, father, and Fiona rotated shifts with the child. The house seemed always occupied by doctors or police or detectives. And Percy screamed and wailed interminably. If he was put down for a nap, he screamed until someone picked him up. If he was put down to play, he screamed until Fiona, Mother or Father either sat beside him or held him.

And when he grew, walked, then ran, he climbed all over the furniture, even on the grand piano. If someone weren't watching him every minute, he'd sneak away and go into the bedrooms where he'd cause havoc by emptying out drawers. And once, the very worst time, when Emalyn was left to watch over him, she turned to put a batch of chocolates into the oven, and he disappeared. Emalyn found him in the parlor, relieving himself on the expensive rug.

As hard as she tried not to, she came to dislike him immensely.

Several times, Emalyn had gone to her bedroom to find the boy perched in the green chair digging at the cushion. Horrified that he might discover her treasure, Emalyn insisted on a lock for her bedroom door, one that she could lock from the outside. Her father complied, and Emalyn relaxed...until Percy's ninth birthday when she went upstairs, saw her door ajar, and found him going through the drawers in her room. She immediately looked at the velvet chair. The cushion lay on the floor, ripped in several places by a pair of scissors that lay on the floor.

Emalyn screamed. When her screams brought her father, mother, Fiona and even her young friend Owen into her room, the group found Percy sitting on the side of Emalyn's bed smiling sweetly, and Emalyn crumpled in a heap beside her chair. Her father wrapped his arms around her and cooed, "Be still, my little one. Be still. Papa's here now."

"I tried to lock him out, but he found a way in," Emalyn said between sobs.

Her father stood, then and turned to the boy.

"Percy, you will go downstairs with your mother where you will stay. You are forbidden entry into any of the rooms upstairs. Do you understand me, boy?"

Percy sat stone still on the side of the bed.

"He's ruined my chair, Mama," Emalyn said. "My green velvet chair."

Then, Emalyn picked up the scissors and held them for Fiona and her mother and father to see.

"This is what that mind of his thinks about. Destruction."

Young Owen walked over to Percy and held out a hand.

"Come along, boy," he said firmly.

During the next week, her mother bought fabric for her to mend the velvet chair, so she carefully recovered the cushion, grateful to God that her treasure was still there. She spent long hours in her room, and though she'd protected her treasure again from Percy, she didn't seem to be able to relax. Deep inside, she felt that nothing in her room would ever be safe from him again.

He'd changed everything.

Fiona cried more, talked less, and seemed cold and distant when she spoke.

Mother was given to fits of temper and spent more time outside than inside, sometimes not even coming in for dinner.

Father worked longer hours and seemed to carry the weight of the world on his shoulders. Often, when he stopped in to say good-night before bedtime, he'd enter her room with a frown but when he turned to her, a thin smile came to his lips…a forced smile, not his usual loving Papa smile.

Their happiness as a family had been replaced with tension and strain.

The only one who hadn't changed was Owen. He was always his optimistic self, seeing Percy's acts as nothing more than childish mischief.

Emalyn sighed. "Forget the past. Think of the present," she chided herself.

She thought of the way Owen was always so protective of Percy, always willing to see the good buried inside him, and for the first time in a long time, she felt sorry for the boy.

"Angels protect him," she whispered.

She was quiet for a moment, and then her thoughts turned to the celebration. Tonight, she had a gift for Owen, one that would make him happy. She went to the closet and took down a square box wrapped in glittering gold paper and tied with large yellow bows. Then she opened the bedroom door, looked up and down both sides of the hallway, leaned over the railings and peered into the downstairs foyer.

When she was sure that Owen was otherwise occupied, she hurried down the stairs and ducked into his study. She placed the box in the middle of his desk, shut the door quietly behind her, and headed back upstairs to do some last-minute touch-ups to her hair and makeup. In the formal dining room behind her, she heard Owen talking with some of the guests and smiled. He'd not seen her.

Once in the bedroom, she studied her appearance. The lovely gown overshadowed the stray wisps of hair that had fallen away from her chignon. Her makeup wasn't perfect, but it would do since she didn't want to bother adding any more. And the final touch was her gloves, there on the bed waiting to be slipped onto her hands and arms. Long, white and pure satin, the elbow-length gloves had belonged to her mother. She slid them on and admired her reflection.

She was about to leave when she heard barking.

A dog? But, we haven't any dog.

When the bark came a second time, Emalyn walked to the balcony and looked down through the front garden and across the road.

On the side of the road opposite their front lawn stood a beggar. He wore a long, tattered black coat, a dark knitted hat pulled down around his ears, and a worn pair of brown Wellies. Beside him, an enormous dog sat, his mouth open, his tongue hanging out, his tail swishing back and forth in the dirt.

Instinctively, she stepped back.

When she did, the beggar bowed low then looked at her and grinned.

Emalyn shuddered.

5

The Celebration

Emalyn stood at the top of the enormous staircase waiting for Owen.

Just then, she saw him with a good sized bundle wrapped in burlap. He handed it to one of the male guests and whispered something in his ear. The man patted Owen on the shoulder and left out the front door.

"Ah, my swan," Owen called to her from the bottom of the steps. "My lovely swan."

The guests had all gathered in the foyer.

Owen met her at the top of the stairs, laid her gloved hand atop his, and guided her down and into the foyer. Immediately, the guests swarmed around her, admiring the beautiful gown, carefully touching the floral chiffon and the silk roses at her waist.

"You look like a vision, Emalyn," they said. "This dress is absolutely stunning!"

"It was his anniversary gift to me," Emalyn said and put her hand on Owen's arm. "He has such impeccable taste."

"One need only look at his choice of brides to know that," someone said.

Emalyn felt the heat rising in her cheeks.

"Still the blushing bride," her friends said.

The sound of their hearty laughter filled the house.

Emalyn felt as if she'd never been happier. She looked up at Owen, ran her hand along his smooth cheek.

"Isn't it wonderful?"

"Beyond wonderful, my love," he said.

Emalyn glanced behind him at a sofa table piled high with brightly colored boxes.

"Oh, dear," she said. "We asked them not to bring gifts but to donate to the orphanage instead."

"Many of them did, I hear," Owen said, "according to the Mother Superior. It was quite a large sum that will enable them to buy much of what they need for all of the children. But some people love to give gifts, my dearest. You can't deny them the pleasure."

"You're right, of course. Now, tell me, what was in that burlap bag you gave to the Senator?"

Just then, Fiona appeared in the doorway of the dining room. She held a crystal bell and rang it three times.

"Happy Evening to all of you," Owen said, his voice ringing like a song throughout the foyer. "Please join us for our anniversary celebration dinner."

The happy throng filed into the massive formal dining room, its hallmark an ornate escutcheon from which hung a sparkling five-tiered chandelier. Two large tables were perfectly adorned with sterling silver candelabras, gold-edged china, gold flatware, and glittering crystal. Fresh flowers in crystal vases formed the centerpieces of each table.

"Elegant as usual," someone said to Emalyn. "Perfectly beautiful. No detail left unattended."

"You may thank our Fiona for her mastery of table settings," Emalyn said.

They feasted on heaping portions of roasted beef, pork sausages, mashed potatoes with cheese, spiced cabbage, warm brown bread with homemade jam...Fiona's version of farm fare. For dessert, Fiona had made her famous double-crusted brandy apple tarts topped with whipping cream, and for the special touch, a piece of Emalyn's elegant chocolate candy.

"Owen, my man," Councilor Murphy said, "I'm not sure I've ever had a better meal. Congratulations to you and Emalyn, and many thanks to Fiona. By the way, Emalyn, these chocolates are heavenly."

"Oh, I agree," said Councilor Quinlan's wife Mariana. "The white swans are so delicate and delicious."

Others chimed in extolling the pleasures of Emalyn's little chocolate candies.

Finally, Bishop Hanrahan said, "Emalyn, dear, have you considered opening a shop?"

"A shop, Bishop?"

"Yes, right here in Dungarran. Why, I think you could single-handedly put our little hamlet on the map, so to speak. People adore your chocolates, and we need more businesses here. We'd all help with the advertising. You could build quite a following, perhaps even worldwide if we did our jobs as marketers."

"How very strange," Emalyn said. "Just this afternoon, I mentioned to Fiona that someday I'd like to have a little chocolate shop."

"Wonderful! You should consider it in greater detail, then, Emalyn dear. You know, the old candy shop, like so many of our former businesses, has been abandoned for years since the..." The Bishop stopped.

"The bombing," Owen said. "Yes, we remember, Bishop."

"Well," said the rotund Bishop, leaning back in his chair, "the old place has been sitting there all this time going to ruin. We have fine carpenters, electricians and plumbers who would be happy to help restore it. It would benefit the workers and bring back some life to the town. These candies would bring in a fair price. You could donate both the unused candies and extra funds to the orphanage, perhaps."

Emalyn straightened in her chair and smiled.

"Oh, that would be lovely."

Owen patted her hand.

"Of course, my love, the Bishop is right. It is something to consider."

With a bit of effort, the aging Bishop stood and cleared his throat.

"Well, then," he said as he raised his glass of wine, "a toast to the lovely couple's third wedding anniversary and, perhaps, to the future first anniversary of Lady Emalyn's Chocolates."

All of the guests toasted then stood and applauded.

"Seems the town is supporting you," Owen whispered to her. "They've even named the place for you."

"To Lady Emalyn's Chocolates," several of the guests cried.

Emalyn glanced at Councilor Quinlan's wife, Mariana, a lifelong friend. Mariana nodded at her and smiled.

But Councilor Murphy's wife, Pearl, another lifelong friend, stared at Emalyn and mouthed "No." Then she closed her eyes and lowered her head.

Emalyn wrapped her hand around Owen's.

"Whatever is wrong?" Owen asked as he leaned in toward her, a look of deep concern on his face. "You're trembling, darling."

Her reply was simply to squeeze his hand.

Owen gave her a brief tight hug then stood.

"We thank you all," he said, "for joining us in the celebration of this, our third anniversary. There is no gift better than the company of cherished friends...except perhaps the love of an extraordinary woman. A final toast, if you will, to Dungarran's own and my most adored wife, the Lady Emalyn Dunaghy Meade."

With the final toast, the guests milled about for only a few minutes and then left for their own homes. When the house was quiet again, Emalyn leaned back in her chair and rested her head on the cushioned back.

"Thank you," she said. "You always manage to handle things so beautifully."

"Come, my love," Owen said and smiled. "Let us retire to our private sanctuary."

"But I should help Fiona clear away these dishes," she said. "She can't do all of this by herself. It isn't right."

"Then we'll both help and make short work of it."

When the table was cleared, the dishes loaded into the new Hydro-Electric dish washing machine, and the food safely stored away, Fiona bid them good night with a kiss on the cheek for each.

"Happy Anniversary," she said. "I've never known two people more suited for one another. God smiled on us there. Now, go on with ya. 'Tis tired you must be and me with you. Sweet sleep."

They headed towards the staircase, but Emalyn stopped.

"I almost forgot," she said. "Come with me into your study."

Emalyn giggled when Owen raised his eyebrows.

The gaily-wrapped box sat in the middle of the desk.

"Open it."

Owen carefully unwrapped the gift. As he admired the painting of his mother and father framed in ornate gold, Emalyn saw his eyes well with tears.

"How did you do this? Where did it come from? I...I never thought I'd see them again."

"I found a tiny snapshot years ago, my love. Jean Pierre, our French artist friend, has been working on it for two years. He did a lovely job, don't you think? We'll hang it wherever you want."

"You are magnificent," he said and put his arm around her narrow shoulders. Then he released her and walked to the radio cabinet.

When Bing Crosby began to sing, "Good Night, Sweetheart," they swayed in time with the music, and when the song had finished, they stayed together in a tight embrace.

Without warning, Owen gathered her up in his arms and headed upstairs.

"To our private chamber, m'lady," he said.

Emalyn tilted her head back and squealed with delight.

• • •

At two in the morning, Emalyn was locked in a world of terror.

She saw herself as a child of six standing outside as a storm raged around her. Thunder boomed so loudly that the ground shook. Dark gray clouds rolled above. The wind howled and whipped the ends of her loose hair against her forehead and chin. Raindrops pelted her face like stinging wasps.

She heard her mother's frantic call. But the voice sounded far away, and Emalyn felt riveted in place, entranced by a spark of white light that danced in the sky. It whispered to her in a muffled sound of jumbled words.

Another blast of thunder shook the ground. Emalyn flailed her arms to keep her balance and took a few steps forward toward the shimmering light and the voice she couldn't quite understand.

The sky had turned almost black now, and as she watched, the spark of light traveled directly to her. It streaked down from the darkness above and struck the ground between her small feet. She saw her shoes blacken, felt a sting on the bottom of her feet, and heard a loud hum in her ears.

And then he appeared.

"Emalyn, run. Run for safety," he said.

She looked at the form in front of her but could not run. He stood so tall she could barely see his face. Gold bands encircled both arms, and his enormous white wings moved gently behind him.

"Run, Emalyn," he said again, and this time, Emalyn saw the beautiful face, the waves of dark hair. From all around him shone a brilliance that reminded her of halos she'd seen in picture books.

He reached down to her and put his warm hand on the top of her head. Emalyn gasped at the heat that traveled through her body. Then, he removed his hand and nudged her shoulder.

"Run," he said. "Run now."

"But who...who are you?" Emalyn asked.

He spoke and Emalyn recognized the voice she'd heard earlier.

"Your guardian," he said.

"What is your name?"

He whispered a name she didn't understand. Emalyn reached out to touch him, her fingers brushing against a wing.

And then, almost against her will, she turned away. Her feet moved, and she ran in the direction of her house. She paused and turned around, but he was gone. Where the two of them had stood, smoke rose in billows. Emalyn smelled burning meat. Blood dripped onto her hands. She reached up and felt a deep gash in her forehead.

Then, all at once, she was afraid, and before she could stop herself, she screamed.

Owen gathered her into his arms.

"All is well, my love," he said as he rocked back and forth and rubbed her back. "It was just the dream again. You're safe, darling, safe."

And even though Emalyn knew it had been only a dream this time, she knew, too, that it happened exactly as it had when she was six, when the lightning strike had burned her body, and when she saw her magnificent angel for the first time.

6

The Beggar

From the black velvet pouch, Emalyn gently lifted the cherished strand of her mother's pearls and held them to her cheek. Today, especially, she needed the steady strength of her dear mother.

"I miss you, Mama," she whispered and kissed the pearls.

As she clasped them around her neck, she thought back to the anniversary celebration a few nights ago. The look on her friend Pearl's face had unnerved her. All of her other friends seemed delighted with the prospect of the chocolate shop, but Pearl alone had mouthed, "No." She wondered why and decided she'd stop by her house on the way home.

Today, she was meeting with the city council to hear their ideas for re-establishing a business in the old candy shop. Owen would be there since he was Vice President of the council.

Emalyn pulled open the doors of her massive mahogany wardrobe.

"Ah, yes," she said, "the new one, the Chanel," she said as the removed the green silk dress from its place and laid it on the bed. She admired the lace along the hem and around the pointed collar. To complete the outfit, she chose bone-colored pumps with a thick heel and straps high along the top of her foot. She chose her new bone-colored hat tilted to one side and pulled netting down carefully over her forehead. Then she adjusted the pink silk roses on the narrow brim , and chose a matching sweater embroidered along the sleeves with pink roses.

Fiona stuck her head in the door. "Need anything, my girl?"

"Come in and tell me what you think of this outfit. Will it be fine for my meeting today?"

Emalyn watched as Fiona surveyed her choices.

"I think it's all perfect," she said. "The touch of pink on the sweater will be lovely, and that dark green color will look just wonderful with your red hair. Good choice, dear."

Emalyn wound a loose curl or two around her fingers.

"Did you notice that all of my friends have those short cuts? Maybe I should consider..."

"Nonsense," Fiona interrupted. "Your hair's always been soft as silk and just look at the pretty waves. It'd be a shame to cut it."

"Oh, bless you. Then I'll not feel bad about my long hair. Is the braid straight? I thought with the new hat a single braid in back might look smart."

Fiona straightened and tightened the braid.

"We need a wee bit of ribbon," she said as she rummaged through the bureau. "Here we go."

She brought a thin strip of pink ribbon and tied it at the end of the braid.

"Now, then, it's perfect. Just enough without too much. You'd better finish up now so you won't be late for your own meeting," she said and chuckled.

Emalyn dressed, checked her appearance one last time, and walked downstairs.

She stopped three quarters of the way down. A sense of dread washed over her. Of all the people she expected to see this morning, he was not one of them.

Percy stood at the door with a silly grin on his face. The swelling had gone down in his eye, and he seemed physically improved.

Emalyn reached the bottom step and nodded at him.

"I trust you're feeling better," she said. She could hear the cold tone of her voice and knew he recognized it, too.

She reached for the door handle, but the boy jumped ahead of her and opened the door.

"Have a nice day," he said, "and say hello to Councilor Murphy for me."

"Councilor Murphy? How do you know him? Why would..."

"Percy!" Fiona called. "Come along with ya, now. You'll be late for school."

The twelve-year-old dashed off in the direction of the kitchen. About halfway there, he turned and grinned at Emalyn.

She stared after him, her heart beating a bit faster, her hands trembling ever so slightly.

Oh, get a hold of yourself. He's just a boy.

She closed the door behind her and stood for a moment on the large front porch admiring Fiona's handiwork with the brightly-colored potted plants. She brushed at her skirt and headed down the walkway.

Bright green hedges lined both sides and in several places in the large yard, she and her mother and Fiona had planted circles of rose bushes: pink, coral, and yellow. They'd burst into bloom a few months ago and filled the land with brilliant color. In the center of the right side of the lawn was the pond capped with green marble, now full of water lilies. And on the opposite side stood a four-tiered marble fountain, ornately carved and topped with an angel, wings spread as if he were about to take flight. Her father had commissioned it the first year they'd lived at Dunaghy Manor. He always had a fondness for angels.

Along the perimeter of Dunaghy Manor, several rowan trees stood like sentinels.

Emalyn opened the tall wrought iron gate and stepped onto the narrow dirt road that led to Dungarran, a small town made even smaller since the tragic bombing four years ago.

Emalyn shook her head and took a deep breath. She imagined how her little shop might look, the way she'd arrange the counters and the displays. She might have a weekly special featuring an exotic chocolate recipe. And of course, what she didn't sell each day would go to those who couldn't afford to buy the candies. She thought about what she'd call the shop and decided on a name: Swans. She would ask Owen what he thought of it when they met today at the old library. Then she reminded herself again that she needed to see Pearl.

The library was her favorite building, the only one in town that had been left in its original stone color. At its entrance sat two lions on short stone columns capped with green Connemara marble. The steps leading to the doors, also done in green marble, gave the building a look of royalty as if some grand family lived within.

Emalyn walked along the dirt road content with her images of Dungarran and excited about the new possibilities in her life. Her new shoes seemed to take the rough roads quite well. She hadn't stumbled a single time and the shoes felt comfortable on her feet. They were, in fact, similar to the ones she'd worn at her wedding three years ago, though the heels of her wedding shoes were narrower and higher.

She could see herself standing beside Owen in the St. Patrick's Cathedral, filled almost to capacity with their friends and relatives. Her dress, white and shimmering, made her feel like a queen. Fiona and several of the best seamstresses from Dungarran and the surrounding villages had worked on it for a year. The satin bodice shone with hand beading that traveled down each of the long, sheer sleeves and formed bracelets at each wrist. The back, very low cut, had a jewel-encrusted band across the center with teardrop crystals cascading to her waist. The lace overlay, imported from Carrickmacross—where the finest Irish lace was handmade—floated down the full satin skirt and formed a six-foot train.

The attendees gasped as she walked down the aisle, and long after the wedding was over, people commented to her that it was the most beautiful dress—and she, the most elegant bride—that Dungarran had ever produced.

A barking dog interrupted her reverie.

Startled, she stumbled on a large stone in the road but managed not to fall.

"May I help ya there, Ma'm?"

Emalyn clutched her chest.

Directly in front of her stood the beggar she'd seen a few days ago. He wore the same tattered black coat, a knit cap pulled down over his ears, and dirty Wellies. And though he was much taller than she recalled, his shoulders broader and straining against the coat, she knew he was the same man. Beside him sat the enormous panting dog, tail swishing in the dirt, tongue lolling out.

Still clutching at her chest, she walked a few steps forward along the road.

"Scraps for Mr. Jones, Ma'm?" the beggar called. "He's hungry, he is."

Emalyn stopped. She wanted nothing to do with this man. He made her nervous, yet she couldn't figure out why. Perhaps he was not a beggar at all but a thief of some sort…or worse, a murderer. She shuddered at the thought.

"Please, Lady, just a few scraps for Mr. Jones?" he said in a soft gentle voice.

In spite of her misgivings and nerves, Emalyn turned to face him.

The beggar lowered his eyes.

"So, that's your name, Mr. Jones? I don't recall any people named Jones in our part of Ireland."

"No'm, not mine. This is Mr. Jones," he said and scratched the dog's head.

"The dog?"

The dog barked and took a few steps in her direction. Emalyn backed away from the giant beast.

"He'll not harm ya, Lady. Mr. Jones is a king among dogs. He's a big 'un but mostly gentle as one of the Father's own lambs. Mostly."

"And what is your name, then?"

The beggar mumbled something she couldn't understand.

"I beg your pardon?"

"Well, you see, Ma'm, it's not important. It's my dog who needs help."

The fact that he wouldn't share his name made her heart's rapid pace quicken all the more.

Something's not right.

"Me and Mr. Jones is lookin' for some work."

The beggar continued to scratch the dog's head.

"Then, wouldn't you fare better in town?"

"Not much call in town for our skills," the beggar said.

The beggar and the dog seemed to be moving closer. Only a few seconds ago, they were at least six feet away. Now, they were so close she could feel the dog's breath as he panted.

Emalyn stepped back.

"What sort of work do you do?"

For the first time, the beggar looked at her square in the eyes.

"We find things," he said. "Me and Mr. Jones find treasures. Ain't that right, Mr. Jones?"

The dog whined and held up a paw. The beggar bent and shook the paw.

Emalyn could hear her heart beating all the way up to her ears where it throbbed like loud drum beats.

My treasure? I touched it this morning. It's safe. It must be. It must be. I have to get rid of him, get him out of here.

Hands still trembling, she reached into her handbag and drew out a sack which held an apple, an orange, cheese slices, brown bread, and a few slices of roast pork.

"Here," she said and tossed it to the beggar. "You'd best be moving on now. There's no treasure here."

"There's treasure everywhere, Ma'm. You just have to look for it. We thank you, but we'd be mighty grateful if you'd..."

"I'm late for a meeting. Please move on."

Emalyn hurried up the road to the town center of Dungarran, her heart still hammering in her chest, her hands still shaking. She saw Owen waiting just as she crested the hill. She ran to him and threw her arms around his neck.

"Oh, Owen, thank goodness."

Owen hugged her to him and kissed her on the cheek.

"What's wrong? What's upset you so?"

"Did you see him? Him and that dog?"

"Who do you mean?"

"The beggar, of course, and Mr. Jones, his dog. They were in front of the house."

"But darling, they're harmless, aren't they? The poor man needs work like so many of our citizens here. That's all."

Emalyn unwrapped herself from Owen and stepped back.

"No, that's not true. For one thing, he isn't a citizen here. He told me he was a treasure hunter. We've never had beggars at Dunaghy Manor. Never. Why would he come here of all places? Why not go into town?"

Owen put an arm around her shoulders.

"It will be all right, Emmy. He's just a beggar. I'll confess to you now that this is partly my fault. I gave him some scraps the other night. I felt sorry for him and that huge old dog of his. I just couldn't hold back food from him when we had so much."

He kissed the top of her head.

"But I'll send him away if I see him again. Worry yourself not, darling. I promise I will take care of it."

"Promise?"

"I won't have you upset by anyone. So, when I see him, I will tell him to leave this area. He won't be bothering you again, my love."

"Oh, Owen, I don't know what I'd do without you."

She looked up to see her dashing husband smiling down at her.

"You are my swan," he said. "My mate for life. Without you, I'd not want to draw another breath."

Emalyn took his hand in hers and kissed it. "Don't talk of death, darling. Not that. No…I can't think of how I would exist without you. I wouldn't want to live, Owen….no, please don't talk about it."

"Shh," he said and held her close. He lifted her chin and kissed her forehead, both cheeks, then her lips. The kiss was soft and loving at first but grew longer and more passionate.

"I love you, Emmy," he said. "Don't be afraid. The two of us are one for eternity. Now, where is that beautiful smile I love?"

She smiled at him.

They walked in silence until they reached the town.

The cobblestone roads of High Street were Emalyn's favorite. Mostly worn smooth by now, they signaled something akin to home for her. Main Street, typical in any Irish towns close to a major waterway, was paved now, but in years past, it was a dirt road that served as the thoroughfare for cattle and sheep.

And every once in a while when the River Shannon overflowed, the water gushed down Main Street and into the River Erne…while business could be conducted as usual on High Street.

High Street, safe from herds of cattle and rushes of water, was the town center. Two and three-story buildings lined the cobblestone path. Brightly painted in bold blues, reds, corals, and pinks, they gave Dungarran the familiar Irish look she'd missed so much when they lived in London, a dark and grey place, the opposite of her family's beloved Ireland.

When they reached the steps of the old library where the meeting was to take place, Owen turned away from her and looked up.

"Storm's coming," he said.

And at that moment, the wind whipped around them, the sky darkened, and the rain poured in icy sheets.

The Meeting

The eleven board members rose when the couple walked in.

"Ah," Councilor Murphy said, "here they are, our esteemed Vice President and his lovely wife. Please, sit down and join us."

Owen held Emalyn's chair for her and patted her on the shoulder.

When the Bishop had finished with his opening prayer, Emalyn saw him look at her briefly. He seemed to want to say something, but then, he lowered his eyes and made a swift exit.

She shifted in her seat and smoothed her skirt.

The President of the Board, Dr. Maquire, explained the business terms of the agreement to use the old candy shop.

"We have electrical workers, water service experts, and craftsmen ready to begin the renovations and installations," he said. "I'd say you could plan to set up the chocolate shop within sixty days, if that meets with your approval. The city will sponsor you so that we will absorb all installation and renovations charges since Dungarran owns the building proper. From that point, the cost of electricity and water or any additions or changes you wish to make will be your responsibility."

"Does that sound fair, Lady Emalyn," Dr. Maquire said.

"It does, Mr. President," she said, "but we haven't discussed the specific amounts of rental and estimates of the monthly charges for electric and water service. It will be a new business. The cost of operating..."

"Rental costs are low and services are minimal, as I've already discussed at length with our Vice President," Dr. Maquire said and nodded at Owen.

Emalyn felt as if she'd been dismissed.

"Gentlemen," Owen said and scooted his chair back. "Please give me a moment to confer with my wife."

When they were out in the hall and sure no one else was around, Emalyn said,

"I should like to have known the costs involved. I have never run a business. What if I don't succeed?"

"Well, now," her husband said, his back straight, arms folded across his chest, "I have every faith that your business will be successful. Dr. Maguire is right. The services and rent are minimal, and you will show a profit. People adore your chocolates."

"But what if the business fails, Owen? Will we be ruined?"

He put his large hand on her cheek.

"No, my love," he said. "We will not be ruined. Our finances are well beyond what this business venture could possibly use. We each have healthy inheritances, our manor is paid for, and we owe very little. I had no idea you were so concerned."

"Oh, Owen," she said, "how do you do it?"

"Do what?"

"Oh, you...you have the power to make me feel safe and secure, always, no matter what happens."

He bent down and kissed her softly on the lips.

"Whatever I do for you, I do out of love. You are my swan, after all."

"Tell me one more time," she said. "Just one more."

49

Owen hugged her tightly to him and whispered, "I am the sun. You are the moon. I die gladly each night just so you can breathe."

Emalyn sighed and snuggled as close to him as she could get. His strong arms and broad chest were like a warm and comforting feather bed into which she could sink and relax.

"I would stay like this forever, love," Owen said, "but we have a meeting to finish, a deal to make."

She stepped away.

"Come on then, will you?" she said. "Let's not keep the board members waiting."

Owen shook his head and chuckled.

An hour or so later, with terms further explained and documents signed, Emalyn walked out of the library holding Owen's hand.

She halted abruptly.

"I forgot something. I meant to ask Councilor Murphy about Percy."

"Percy?"

"As I left this morning, Percy opened the door for me."

"He did? What on earth came over him?"

"He told me to tell Councilor Murphy hello for him."

Owen put his hand under his chin and ran an index finger across his lip.

"Hmm," he said. "To my knowledge, the only contact the two of them have had has been quite negative. It was the Councilor who threatened him with expulsion if he was caught fighting with the older gangs again."

Emalyn sighed.

"That boy is such a mystery," she said. "Why does he hang around with such rough people? There are plenty of nice young boys and girls his age at school."

"Yes, but Percy gets the sharp end of the stick most of the time because of his limp."

"Wait one moment," she said and ran to talk to the Councilor.

"Councilor Murphy," she called. "A moment of your time, please."

He turned and smiled at her.

"Emalyn, what is it that I can do for our newest business owner?"

"I wanted to tell you about Percy."

The councilor coughed several times as if he'd chocked on something.

"Are you all right?"

He cleared his throat.

"Yes, fine," he said, his face considerably reddened. "Must have a nasty cold coming on. You wanted to ask me about Fiona's boy?"

"Yes, this morning, he told me to tell you hello. I thought it was a bit odd, that's all. He's never mentioned you before."

"Hmm," the Councilor said, "perhaps our little confrontation on Friday made an impression. I cautioned him severely about all this fighting. He was quite angry with me, so perhaps he was being a bit sarcastic this morning."

Emalyn nodded. "Perhaps."

Just then, she heard Owen call to her.

"I'll go now. Maybe we can discuss this a bit more at a later date," Emalyn said.

"Oh, certainly. Right now, though, you should be concentrating on that new shop."

Emalyn smiled and hurried away to meet Owen.

"Did you ask him?"

"Yes," Emalyn said as they walked outside. "Apparently there was some confrontation on Friday. He'd reprimanded Percy for fighting."

Owen frowned.

A group of men stood at the bottom of the stairs. They looked like a ragtag bunch with tattered clothing, greasy hair, scruffy beards, and worn out boots.

"Speaking of ruffians," Emalyn whispered.

She recognized all of the men as farmers who lived down the road from Dunaghy Manor.

"Gentlemen," she said as she and Owen walked past them. "Good day."

The tallest among them stood in front. He nodded at her. "I'm sure it's always a good day for the Lady," he scoffed.

The others chuckled.

"Excuse us," Owen said as he took Emalyn by the elbow.

"Ain't no excuse for the likes of you," their speaker yelled.

"Yeah, that's right," the others shouted.

"What do they mean?" Emalyn whispered, her heart racing.

Owen stopped and motioned for her to sit on one of the benches. He turned to face the group.

"Please, gentlemen," he said. "My wife has nothing to do with your complaint against the Board."

"Oh, don't she, now?" the speaker of the bunch said and took a few steps toward Owen. "She's opening a business, ain't she? Gonna be using the electric and water services? Course, with somebody like her, it don't make no difference. Miz Moneybags. What bother is it to her to pay huge sums for somethin' she didn't want in the first place?"

In spite of her rising fear, Emalyn could not stay seated.

"What are you talking about?" she said calmly and walked up beside Owen. "What does my business have to do with you? You're farmers with your own businesses."

"We're farmers, all right, but our businesses belong to this fine country of Ireland, and probably England, too if anyone knew the truth? We pay for the right to work and use their electrics and water, and we didn't want it in the first place. We were doin' fine 'til this electric and water board came down on us so heavy. Yeah, we got electric. We got water from the city, but we can't afford neither of 'em. So now we got nothin'. Every penny we make goes to pay for the water and electric we didn't even want or need. The greedy sons of..."

Owen interrupted.

"But all of you signed the petition years ago for electric and water, all of you."

"And what if we hadn't? What then? We had no choice," one of the shorter ones yelled, shaking his fist in the air. "It was either sign or close down. We was lied to and cheated out of our money by these greedy..."

"We'll destroy any new businesses here for supporting the devil who runs this board," the leader said and spat on the ground at Emalyn's feet.

Emalyn stepped back.

Owen moved in front of her.

"I'd ask you to leave now," Owen said, his voice stern. "My wife is not to be bothered."

The gang of men guffawed.

"Oh, ain't she pitiful, now. If she opens that business, you can bet she'll be bothered. Anybody who supports those money-grabbin' devils will be run off."

Owen moved closer to the men and put his index finger close to the leader's face.

"I'll not have you speaking to her in such a way."

"And what are ya gonna do about it, now?"

Owen balled his fists.

"Shall we settle this in the alley, then?"

Emalyn gasped. Though she knew Owen was a powerful fighter, he was grossly outnumbered.

From the top of the stairs a voice boomed across them.

"Johnny Macahern!"

The group of men looked up to see Councilor Murphy descending the steps, his face red with anger.

"What in heaven's name do you men think you're doing?"

"It ain't fair, Councilor," Johnny said. "It ain't fair that we're forced to use the electric and water and pay you for being farmers. It ain't right."

"And you think the Lady Emalyn can help with that?"

"We don't need no new businesses supportin' you bunch of thieves on the Board. The more support you've got, the more the poor people in this county suffer."

The Councilor leaned close to the leader, Johnny.

"Get your gang of ruffians out of here. Loitering is a crime, and I'll see that you're fined if I so much as hear a whisper about you pulling this kind of stunt again. Leave that woman alone. Now, get out of here, all of you!"

The disgruntled group moved away muttering and spitting. Then, the leader turned around and pointed a finger at them.

"You'll pay for this, ya know? Just like before."

Emalyn stepped closer to Owen whose hands were still balled into fists, jaw firmly set, mouth in a tight line.

"What does he mean?"

She tugged at his arm, but he didn't budge.

"Please, love, let it go. They did no harm," she said.

She tugged again, and he seemed to snap out of his rage. He wrapped his arms around her.

"In my eyes," he said, "they did harm when they spoke to you so rudely. I won't have it, Emmy."

"Come," she said. "Let's go home. We'll have a bit of lunch before you have to go back to the factory. Heroes need their strength, after all."

"I'm no hero, Emmy."

"Ah, but there you're wrong. You are always my hero," she said and hugged tightly to his arm as they walked.

When they'd gone only a few paces, Emalyn asked again.

"But what did they mean? Just like before? And why will the poor suffer?"

Owen turned to face her.

"I'm afraid Johnny is right," he said. "When the Board enacted this Electric and Water Act, the majority of the people thought it was grand. But the farmers didn't want it."

"They didn't want city water and electricity?"

"No, they didn't. They'd made a decent living without it for years."

Emalyn nodded.

"I see," she said. "But they were forced to have the water and electric lines and to pay for them?"

Owen nodded.

"So, all of this is about money," Emalyn said. "The farmers couldn't afford it but were forced to have it. The expenses took away their profits. The new businesses would naturally need it and wouldn't mind paying for it."

"Yes."

Owen held on to Emalyn with one hand and massaged his temple with the other.

"What's wrong, love?"

"We'll talk about this at home, Emmy. Let's just get home."

They picked up their pace and hurried along the road toward Dunaghy Manor.

"Oh," Emalyn said. "I meant to drop by and speak to Pearl."

"Pearl Murphy?"

"Yes, she did not seem in favor of my opening a business, and I wanted to find out why. I'll speak with her tomorrow morning."

They walked in silence until they reached the front gate.

Then, Emalyn heard the barking dog again.

"Oh, dear," she said. "It's that dog, Mr. Jones, and I'm sure the beggar is there, too."

"Good, I might have work for him."

"What?"

Emalyn felt as if her knees would buckle at any moment. She looked at Owen as if she'd never seen him before, some stranger who'd just suggested something horrible.

"No!" she said. "You promised you'd get rid of him."

"I'm asking that you trust me now, Emalyn. He might be just the person I need."

She wrung her hands.

"How could you possibly need him?" she said. "He's a beggar, maybe even a thief. He makes me nervous. I'm sorry, but it's out of the question."

Owen lifted her chin.

"Do you trust me, my swan?"

With his beautiful ice blue eyes fixed on her, Emalyn felt all her resolve melting away.

"I trust you," she whispered. "Yes, I trust you. I love you."

Owen smiled down at her.

"Then, please, trust me now as never before. I have only your safety in mind, love. I promise you that I would never do anything to bring harm to you or the house. So, bear with me, please. Stand beside me knowing that I have only the very best of intentions."

He kissed her softly on the lips.

Emalyn closed her eyes and let the power of his kiss wash over her in a tingling wave of warmth.

Then she watched as Owen walked across the road and knelt beside Mr. Jones and the beggar.

A little shiver passed through her.

New Business

Another blast of thunder shook the ground. The earlier rain had turned into a violent storm and now raged in the night, shaking even the thick windows of Dunaghy Manor.

In her dream, Emalyn flailed against a storm then took a few steps forward, toward the shimmering light and the voice that called to her.

The blue heavens had turned almost black now, and as she watched, the spark of light traveled directly to her. It struck the ground between her small feet, blackened the bottoms of her shoes, and caused a loud humming in her ears.

And then he appeared.

"Run," he said. "Run for safety."

Emalyn's eyes fluttered open and she moaned.

"I know him," she mumbled. "I know him."

A flash of lightning lit up the bedroom.

Awake now, Emalyn turned her head to see Owen sleeping soundly on his side, both hands tucked under her pillow. As quietly as she could, she slipped out of bed and curled up in the green velvet chair, her fingers stroking the stiffened spot where her treasure lay buried in the cushion.

When the lightning flashed again, she marveled at the way the light cast a soft glow on Owen's body illuminating the broad chest, muscular arms and handsome face. His blond hair fell across his forehead.

Her thoughts drifted to her lost baby, a miscarriage she'd suffered during the first year of their marriage, within the first month of her pregnancy. The doctor's pronouncement that she would probably never be able to carry a child to term had devastated both of them, and for months afterward, they had often cried together at night: she because she would not be able to give her husband a child; he because the thought of losing her was too much for him to bear.

He'd whispered this to her often as they drifted off to sleep in each other's arms, and as she closed her eyes and slipped away, she heard his words: "Swans mate for life. If one should die, the other would pass away of a broken heart."

Owen stirred and turned over onto his back, one arm extended over Emalyn's side. She yawned then crawled in beside him. His arm wrapped around her and drew her close to him.

"I've missed you," he whispered.

Emalyn giggled.

"You've been sleeping. You didn't even know I was up."

He turned over and stared down at her.

"And now that you are...."

She giggled again until his hungry kisses silenced her.

As daylight broke and the storm passed, Emalyn woke to see Owen standing in front of the cheval glass mirror adjusting his silk tie. She admired the striking figure he cut in his tan cuffed pants, white collared shirt, and tweed sweater vest.

"How handsome you look this morning," she said and rubbed the sleep from her eyes.

Owen stood back, took a look at himself, and turned to her. Then he walked to the bed, scooped her into his arms and stepped toward the mirror as he lowered her gently to the floor.

"This," he said, standing behind her with his hands on her shoulders, "this is my reason for doing everything. This petite beauty who is my wife and my eternal love."

She put her hands over his.

Owen wrapped her arms around her waist and kissed her gently on the cheek.

"Today is a big day full of surprises for you, my swan."

"Surprises? What kind of surprises?

"Ah, well if I told you, they wouldn't be surprises, eh? Put on your most elegant suit and meet me at the entrance to Dungarran at noon. Bring Fiona, too. She'll be delighted."

"What on earth have you done, Owen?"

"You'll see. Meet me at noon. Now, I'm late. I must leave you for a while."

"Owen, wait."

"Yes, love?"

"I've been thinking about the beggar."

Owen looked at her quizzically.

"I do trust you, and if you say that you have a job for him, then I agree with you. Your judgment about character is always right, so I will trust him as you do. I know you would never do anything to harm us."

Owen hugged her.

"Thank you, my darling. It fills my heart with joy to hear this. You won't regret it, I promise."

"Is there anything I can do to help him?" Emalyn said.

"Just be your sweet self. That will be more than enough."

He was out the door almost before she could blink.

"Fiona," she called. "Will you come up here for a moment?"

Emalyn searched through her wardrobe and chose a herringbone skirt and beige silk blouse.

"You'll need the overcoat. It's windy and cold today," Fiona said. "Can't have you going around without the proper wrap."

"And you'll be needing yours, as well," Emalyn said. "Owen says we are to meet him at the entrance to Dungarran at noon."

"Whatever for?" Fiona said.

Emalyn shrugged.

"Some big surprise for us. We must go."

"Should I prepare a luncheon, do you think?"

"No, he didn't say anything about a luncheon, just that you and I were to meet him at noon wearing our Sunday best. And Fiona, one more thing. You remember the beggar and his dog?"

Fiona frowned.

"Certainly. Up to no good it seems to me."

"Well, I'm not sure what Owen has arranged, but the beggar will be working for us now. So, please see if you can find it in your heart to accept him."

"Working here?" Fiona asked.

"Yes, he'll be staying in the guest house, I assume. Owen has a job for him."

Fiona sighed.

"I suppose if Mr. Owen thinks it's all right then who am I to disagree?"

Emalyn hugged her.

"We must make him feel comfortable," she said.

"Your Owen," she said, "always cooking up something."

"Oh, Fiona, he's a dream of a husband, isn't he? God sent me the best man in the world."

"I think you're right about that. I've never met another like him. Now, let's take a look at that skirt and blouse to see if they need tidying, and what will we do with your hair?"

"Owen likes it loose, so that's the way I'll wear it. Loose under my hat. I think there's enough curl, don't you?"

Fiona ran her fingers through the long red curls cascading down Emalyn's back.

"Ya have curls aplenty, my girl. You'll be stunning as usual."

"As long as Owen thinks I'm beautiful, that's all that matters."

"Well, you're set then, aren't ya? He thinks you're the most gorgeous woman on earth!"

The two of them chuckled.

When Fiona left, Emalyn straightened the bed and tidied the room. She picked up the framed photo of them on their wedding day and thought that they still looked much the same, still smiling and happy. She blew some dust off the edges of the frame and set it back in place on her nightstand.

After a warm bath, she sat at the vanity table and brushed her hair. In spite of her happiness, a deep depression settled over her as she looked at the photo of her mother and father. She picked up the little golden frame and hugged it to her chest. Tears formed in her eyes.

"I'd give anything to see you both, talk to you, wrap my arms around you. Oh, Mama and Papa, I miss you terribly."

She wondered if she would ever stop missing them or if this grief would be with her until the end of her days.

A knock on the door took her thoughts away from her parents. She wrapped her silk robe tightly around her.

"Fiona? You don't have to knock. Come in."

The door opened slowly.

Emalyn frowned and got up.

"Fiona?" she said.

But it was Percy. He was holding a box tied with a bright red ribbon.

"From Mr. Owen," he said, "to take to the noon meeting."

He handed her the box, and though he smiled, something about that smile made Emalyn shudder. She closed the door without a word to him and set the box on the bed.

Something compelled her to look at the green chair. She knelt in front of it and ran her hand over the cushion. Then she sighed.

It is here. It is safe. My treasure.

When she had finished readying herself, she met Fiona downstairs in the foyer.

"Whatever is that you're holding?" Fiona said. "A gift for Mr. Owen, eh?"

"Percy brought it to me a little while ago."

"Percy? But he's in school."

Emalyn looked at Fiona and shook her head.

"He delivered this to me and said it was from Owen and I was to take it to the meeting."

"That boy," Fiona said. "Lord help me. He'll never amount to anything. Mr. Owen would not have taken him out of school to do such a thing."

"Should I take it with us?"

"He's probably wrapped up one of those toads he's so fond of. But let's take it and show it to the Mister. See what he says."

As they opened the front door, Emalyn stood in shock at what she saw. She put her hand to her chest and fingered the strand of pearls.

"Yes? May we help you?"

The tall man dressed in an expensive suit bowed at the waist. His long hair was slicked stylishly back and tied at the neck. His face, clean shaven and quite handsome, reminded Emalyn of someone.

"I am here to escort you to the meeting," he said.

"Are...are you...the beggar?" Emalyn said. "You are, aren't you?"

When he straightened, again, he seemed taller than she'd remembered, much taller and more handsome with broad shoulders like Owen's.

Fiona stood with her mouth open.

Then, Emalyn heard a dog barking.

"My friend, Mr. Jones," the beggar said. "He looks quite nice since his bath."

The enormous dog sat and held up a paw.

"He'd like a shake, Lady Emalyn, if it doesn't frighten you too much. He's mostly a kind and gentle soul."

Emalyn bent and took the dog's paw in her hand. Instantly, she felt warm and comfortable all over. She relaxed and felt no fear at all.

"Good morning to you, Mr. Jones," she said. "You look very handsome since your bath," she said.

Mr. Jones looked over at the beggar who reached down and patted him on the head.

"Shall we go now?" the beggar asked. Then he reached over and held out a hand. "Allow me to carry the package."

Emalyn handed it to him without a care.

With a sweeping gesture, he stretched out his arm. "Ladies first."

She locked arms with Fiona.

"Thank you very much," Fiona said to him. "We appreciate your help."

Emalyn patted her arm, then stopped and turned around.

"Would you tell us your name, please?" she said to the beggar.

"My name?" he asked.

"Yes, what is your name? I don't want to keep calling you the beggar. A proper gentleman needs a proper name."

Softly, the beggar spoke.

"I am called Jude by my family."

"And would you have a last name?"

"Emalyn!" someone called. "Oh, I'm so glad to see you."

Pearl Murphy walked toward her waving.

"Pearl," she said to her friend. "I've been meaning to stop by."

Pearl hugged her then grabbed Fiona's hand.

"How are you, Fiona? You look lovely today."

Fiona smiled.

"Ladies, if you please. We don't want to be late," the beggar Jude said.

Pearl frowned.

"Now, who might this be?"

"This is Jude," Emalyn said, "and Mr. Jones, his four-legged friend. New to the area."

"You're here on business, then?" Pearl asked.

"Come on," Emalyn said. "Let's get to the meeting before Owen worries that something's happened to us."

As they all crested the hill at the entrance to Dungarran, Emalyn saw a large structure covered in what seemed to be an enormous sheet.

Owen stood in the middle of all of the board members and their wives. The Bishop stood to one side of the group.

Emalyn waved to her husband.

"Ah, there she is, my beautiful bride," he said and kissed her on the cheek. "You're stunning," he said.

"Fiona, Pearl, how nice you both look," Owen said. "And Jude, thank you for escorting the ladies safely here. What is that you have there?"

"Percy gave that to me this morning to bring to the meeting. He said it was from you."

"From me?"

For some reason she couldn't explain, Emalyn felt faint. Her hands trembled, her heart raced, and beads of sweat popped out across her forehead.

Suddenly, behind her, she heard the beggar Jude say, "It's all right, Lady. Sit here," as he scooted a chair under her. "Just relax." He got a chair and offered it to Fiona. "Please, sit beside her."

Fiona sat and rubbed Emalyn's hands.

Mr. Jones, suddenly alert, ears forward, tail straight up, began a low rumbling growl. Within seconds, it turned into a fiercer sound. Then, he darted off like a bolt of lightning and charged into the wooded area surrounding Dungarran's entrance.

"What is wrong with the dog?" Fiona said. "He took off like a shot."

"He'll be back," the beggar Jude said.

The Bishop bent beside Emalyn.

"If you're up to it, we'll begin with a prayer."

When the prayer was done, the board members all gathered around the sheet-covered structure.

"Owen, if you'll do the honors," Councilor Murphy said.

Emalyn watched the one swift movement it took to remove the sheet.

Owen looked at her and said,

"Behold, the Dunaghy-Meade High Cross. Five years ago, our fathers were killed because of this cross, but it was what they wanted to symbolize the economic growth of Dungarran. So, to honor them and all the fine citizens of this town, it stands now as a beacon of growth and prosperity to all who enter here."

Emalyn stood and took a step forward, but the beggar Jude touched her elbow.

"Please, Lady, stay where you are."

She started to protest, but the look in his eyes compelled her to stay.

"The package," Owen shouted in their direction. "Someone has brought a gift to mark this special occasion. Jude, will you bring it?"

The board members applauded when they saw the gold box and bright red bow.

Suddenly, they heard a man scream.

Mr. Jones appeared, his huge mouth clamped around a man's arm. The enormous dog was dragging the man out of the dense forest.

"Johnny Macahern," Councilor Murphy said. "What are you doing here?"

The beggar Jude whistled and Mr. Jones let go of the man and came running back to him. He pointed to where Emalyn stood. "There," he said.

Mr. Jones trotted over and flopped down beside Emalyn, Pearl, and Fiona.

The board members all moved away from the cross, closer to the forested area where Johnny Macahern sat like a whimpering child.

But Owen stood beside his high cross holding the package in his hands.

Pearl called to him, "Owen, wait…please wait."

Emalyn looked at her then turned immediately in Owen's direction, her heart like a hammer in her chest.

"Owen, darling. Wait!"

But Owen focused on untying the bright red ribbon.

The beggar Jude had moved to stand next to him.

When Emalyn tried to run to be beside her love, Mr. Jones blocked her way and nudged her back in her chair.

"Stop it," she yelled at the dog.

The next moments seemed to move silently in slow motion.

The beggar Jude looked over at her and nodded. She hadn't noticed before the soft golden light that surrounded him. He drew back and threw the package. It flew through the air. Then, he wrapped his arms around Owen, hugging him tightly to his chest. Owen glanced at her and mouthed, "I love you."

Emalyn knew something was terribly wrong. She yelled as loudly as she could, "Owen!"

Then a deafening sound blasted through the silence. Emalyn covered her ears. And then, her world turned pitch black.

9

Memorials

A cold nose on her cheek roused Emalyn from a deep slumber. Her eyes fluttered open and she shielded them with her hand against the bright sunlight filtering through the brocade draperies.

She saw Fiona bend down close to her, eyes red and swollen. She whispered, but the whispers sounded odd and far away to Emalyn. Fiona stroked her forehead and kissed her. Emalyn was only vaguely aware of others milling about in her room. Indistinct voices, unintelligible mutterings. The world seemed enveloped in a black fog.

Then she felt a heavy weight beside her on the bed and smiled.

"Owen," she whispered. "I knew you'd be all right."

She closed her eyes, laid a hand on his pillow, and drifted into sleep.

When she opened her eyes again, only her beside lamp shone in the darkness. She ran her hand across Owen's pillow expecting full well to turn and see him sleeping like an angel beside her. Her handsome Owen. Her soul mate. Her...

Emalyn sat straight up and flung the covers back.

"Fiona!" she yelled. "Fiona!"

"I'm here, my girl, right here with ya."

Through her sobs, Emalyn said, "Owen? My Owen?"

"I'm sorry, love," she said. "I'm so sorry."

Fiona sobbed along with her, the two of them slipping to the floor and rocking back and forth in each other's arms.

"It can't be true, Fiona. I felt him in bed just a while ago. I felt him."

"Oh, sweet girl, that was Mr. Jones. He's been by your side since... since the tragedy."

"Fiona, where is my Owen?"

Fiona didn't respond right away.

"Where is he?" Emalyn demanded.

Fiona stroked her hair and her cheeks.

"At the funeral parlor, dearest. Today is the service."

"Today? But it happened only yesterday, Fiona," she said through her sobs. "Only yesterday."

Fiona shook her head. "Was a week ago, my girl."

Emalyn wiped her face with her nightgown.

"I have to see him, Fiona. He's all alone there. He'll want me with him. Will you get my overcoat?"

Fiona struggled up from the floor.

Mr. Jones hopped down from the bed and sat down next to Emalyn. She used his broad back to help herself up. When she stood, the room spun, so she grabbed the big dog's ruff.

Fiona helped her slip on the overcoat and Wellies.

"You've only your gown on, my girl. You can't go out with any clothes. You'll freeze."

But Emalyn didn't care about clothes.

"Find me the scissors, please," Emalyn said. "Hurry."

Emalyn took the scissors and went to the green velvet chair. She plunged the sharp points into the cushion several times.

"What're you doing, Emalyn? You've treasured that chair since you were a girl."

But Emalyn said nothing. She hacked away at the cushion until she could slip her fingers around the small blue box: her treasure.

"I'm going to Owen now," she said and shoved the box into the pocket of her overcoat. As she walked to the door, she stopped. On a small table, she saw a beige envelope with the word *Emalyn* written in gold script.

"What is this?" she said.

"I don't know, love. I haven't seen it before just now," Fiona said.

Emalyn picked it up and turned it over.

"It's still sealed," she said and stuck it into another pocket.

"Then, leave it, my girl. It could be dangerous."

Emalyn shook her head.

Mr. Jones trotted behind her as she hurried down the steps to see her Owen.

A light snowfall and gusty winds made their pace slower, and by the time they reached the funeral house, fine crystals of ice had formed at the edges of Emalyn's hair.

As was customary, the door was kept unlocked so that mourners might come in at their convenience. In spite of the troubles in the town, very few people would ever disrupt the sleeping dead, partly out of superstition that they would be haunted forever, and partly out of respect.

Emalyn and Mr. Jones stepped inside and turned to the right to find the sanctuary as it was called. A dark mahogany casket sat in the middle of the room. Altar lights from behind it cast a golden glow all around it.

Slowly, Emalyn walked forward and saw the body of her Owen. She ran her hand along his cold cheek and kissed his still lips.

"My love," she whispered. "My heart. My life."

From her coat pocket she removed the blue box.

"This will save you, my dearest," she said to Owen. "It saved me long ago, and I'm asking God now to save you, to bring you back to your swan."

She withdrew a single feather from its small container and placed it on Owen's chest.

"It's an angel feather, my love," she said as tears streamed down her cheeks. "An angel saved me from the lightning, and when he left, I held this feather in my hand. I've kept it all these years, hidden it away as a treasure.."

She caressed the white feather.

"Please, God, send your angels to bring back my Owen to me. He is my real treasure, my swan, and I cannot live without him."

Emalyn said again, "Please, please, bring him back to me."

She waited for a sign, any sign, but nothing happened.

Bent almost double in her sobbing, Emalyn slipped down to the floor.

"I've no wish to live without you," she whispered.

Mr. Jones plopped down beside her and put his great head in her lap.

When she reached into her pocket to get a tissue, she felt the envelope. After retrieving it, she broke the seal carefully.

Across the top of the letter was written: *To my swan, my lovely Emalyn, from your beloved.*

Her tears blurred the lines, but she read aloud as best she could in hopes that her Owen might hear her.

> *Now laugh and talk*
> *Of me as if I were*
> *beside you there.*
> *I'd come—I'd come,*
> *could I but find the way!*

But would not tears and grief
be barriers?)
And when you hear a song
Or see a bird
I loved, please do not let
the thought of me
Be sad...For I am
loving you just as
I always have...
Remember that I
did not fear...It was
just leaving you
that was so hard to face
We cannot see beyond
But this I know. I loved you so
Twas heaven here with you.

Emalyn stopped as tears poured down her face. Her heart felt as if it had broken in two pieces, one for her and one for Owen. A hollowness settled inside her, an emptiness, the ache of wanting him close to her. She slumped over and rested her head on the cold floor. Mr. Jones moved up beside her and whined.

"You've lost your friend, too," she said, her breath shallow, her breathing rapid. "The beggar Jude has disappeared. I am sorry for your loss."

Mr. Jones nudged at her hand, and for the first time, she let it rest on his head.

A sensation of warmth suddenly filled her, and she took a deep breath.

"I'm warm now," she said to Mr. Jones. "Stay with me and let me sleep here with my Owen for a while."

She drifted into the needed relief of sleep.

Sometime later, a voice woke her, a far off sound that she could barely hear.

"Lady Emalyn," he said. "I'm no wee angel."

She struggled to open her eyes.

Percy sat on the floor beside Mr. Jones.

"I'm no wee angel, Lady," he said. "I thought you should know."

Emalyn wiped her face and rubbed her eyes, but she couldn't find the strength to sit up.

"What are you talking about?" She could hear the fatigue and weakness in her own voice.

"I'm what you call illeg…illegitimate," he said, his head lowered. "That's what Uncle Johnny says, anyway."

She put her arms across the dog's large back, and he stood carefully, helping her to sit up. She rested her head against the casket.

"What are you trying to tell me, Percy?"

"Them bombs, Lady, weren't never meant for Mr. Owen and your da. They was meant for Councilor Murphy."

"Go on."

"Johnny, he's my uncle, you see. He told me the whole story. My real mam was his sister. But my real pa is Mr. Murphy. Johnny hates him cause he left her and wouldn't pay her no money. But Johnny says my mam didn't want me so he had to feed me. He didn't have no money, either, so he asked Mr. Murphy for some. But Mr. Murphy called him trash and sent him away. So, Johnny, he…"

Mr. Jones nuzzled the boy's hand. Percy bent down and wrapped his spindly arms around him.

73

"I ain't never had no dog," he said.

"Percy, finish the story, please," Emalyn said fighting to keep her eyes open.

"Well, Johnny got real mad at me and…well, he said he hurt me real bad. Then, he took me to Mr. Murphy's house and left me there, but Mr. Murphy, he didn't want me neither, so he left me out on the doorstep at your house."

Emalyn thought of how much Owen had cared for Percy.

"My Owen," she said. "If he cared for you, then I will do the same to honor our love."

She felt Mr. Jones close to her. He nudged his body so that her hands rested on his large back. When her hands began to tingle from the warmth of him, she closed her eyes and took a deep breath. She felt as if a huge weight had been lifted from her.

She opened her eyes, and this time, she saw Percy as a misguided boy, twelve years old, abandoned as a baby by his family, an unwanted little thing beaten and left. More tears streamed down her face.

"Come here, Percy," she said and struggled to her feet bracing herself on the casket.

Through her sobs, she whispered, "I love you, Owen."

She picked up the angel feather and put it back into the box. Then she turned and handed it to Percy.

"It's yours now," she said. "Keep it with you always."

"A feather, ma'am?"

"Yes, a feather. It's from an angel who saved me when I was just a little girl."

"But you might need it still, Lady," Percy said.

"You need it more," Emalyn said. "And you know what it means, don't you?"

Percy shook his head.

"It means that you are very special and that you must always act in a way that will make your angel proud of you."

"No one's ever been proud of me," he said. "Even mam."

"Fiona loves you with all her heart. To make your angel proud, you must love her back. Do what she asks. Stop hurting her with your fighting. Do well in school. Stay away from those gangs, and make up your mind to be of use to the community. If you do all those things, your angel will be very proud and will protect you and smile down at you from Heaven."

Emalyn could feel herself getting weaker, life ebbing slowly away.

"Do you promise me, Percy, that you will always make your angel proud?"

Percy rubbed the blue box against his cheek.

"Yes, Lady, I promise."

"And you must promise to tell your mam all that you've told me. Tell the Bishop as well. Now, can you go and find a pen and paper for me?"

Percy took off to the foyer and returned almost immediately with a pen and paper from the Visitor's Guest Book.

Emalyn managed a weak smile.

Propped against Owen's casket, she wrote until she had no strength left.

Then, with trembling hands, she carefully folded the paper in half.

"I'm very tired, Percy," she said. "Would you help me to the pew so that I can rest?"

When she was comfortable, Mr. Jones once again put his head on her lap.

"Here," she said and handed him the paper. "Give this to your mother. Make sure that you put it in her hands."

"But you will see her in a little while. She'd rather have it from you."

"I'm going to go to sleep for a bit. As soon as your mam comes in, give her that paper. Do you understand?"

Percy nodded.

"And take care of Mr. Jones, too. He'll need a home."

"Are you all right, Lady? You don't look so very good."

But Emalyn had already fallen into a deep sleep, her head resting on the arm of the pew, both hands crossed over her chest and a slight smile on her pale face.

• • •

"Open your eyes, my darling."

Emalyn's eyes fluttered open at the sound of Owen's voice.

"Oh, Owen, my Owen," she sobbed.

He lifted her into his arms.

"Shh," he soothed, "it's all right, love. Everything is all right. We're together, my swan," he said as he covered her face with kisses that dried all her tears.

Emalyn eyes widened. She could hardly believe what she beheld. From her deep sleep, she had stepped into a world of magnificent beauty with striking blue heavens, clouds lined in gold, and colorful gardens that seemed to stretch for miles.

"It's beautiful, isn't it?"

He set her down and smiled.

"Oh, Owen," she said. "You are my treasure, the greatest treasure anyone could have."

"And you are mine. Come, and let me show you our forever home. It is beyond anything you can imagine."

"Owen, am I dead, then?"

"To the world below, yes, but here? No, you are alive in the Kingdom with me."

"But I remember falling asleep and then....hearing your voice."

"That's how it is with the angels, Emmy. When Jude hugged me at the cross, I felt nothing except the warmth of his arms and the sensation of being lifted up."

"Did you miss me?"

Owen didn't answer right away.

"I was at peace here, love. But then, I looked down on you and saw your pain. It grieved me so, but the angels told me to concentrate on preparing a place for you. They said they were helping you."

They walked arm in arm until they reached a lush clearing. Rimmed in golden sheen, the clearing seemed almost alive.

"What is it, Owen?"

"Ah, now you'll see, my swan. I've chosen this spot for us. Now, watch. They'll be coming soon."

Owen pointed to the bright blue heavens. "Do you see them?"

Emalyn turned her face toward the sky. Two winged angels descended slowly to the ground. The taller of the two wore a short white tunic. His muscular arms and legs glistened in the sun. His coal black hair hung below his shoulders, and his sparkling white wings moved in smooth rhythm.

The angel held out both arms at shoulder height, then leaned his head back.

He whispered, but it was a whisper that echoed throughout the clearing.

"Help me, Father, to do your bidding."

The muscles in his arms and legs bulged and strain showed on his handsome face.

"Help me," he whispered again.

A light swooped from the sky and enveloped the angel. It swirled and danced around him in a whirlwind of radiance so bright that she had to shield her eyes.

As quickly as it had come, the light disappeared. The angel dropped to his knees and covered himself with his giant wings.

In the clearing stood a gorgeous house, the very image of Dunaghy Manor. It shone in the sunlight, an iridescent glow pulsing all around. Beside it was a large pond with two swans gliding across."

"Oh, Owen, it's beautiful, so beautiful."

"Our home, my love."

The angel arose joined now by another man similar in appearance. The two walked toward them, huge smiles on their handsome faces, each in a short white tunic. On their muscular arms, they wore bright gold bands and on their feet, golden sandals laced to the knees, but their wings were no longer visible.

When they approached, the taller of the two, the one who had been in the clearing, held out his hand.

"Lady Emalyn," he said. "All is ready."

Emalyn stared at the two for a moment. One seemed familiar but the other…the other was a stranger to her.

The stranger reached to stroke her cheek.

"I am Mr. Jones," he said. "Thank you for sharing your food with me."

"Mr. Jones, the dog?" Emalyn said.

"Well, we do what we must," he replied.

Owen stepped forward and motioned for the other to come closer.

"I am Jude," he said. "Years ago, I met you…"

Emalyn gasped.

"My angel," she said. "When I was six, you saved me from the lightning, and you gave me a feather."

He smiled and nodded.

"I cherished that feather," Emalyn said. "I loved it so much that I never shared it with anyone. I should have shared it with…."

Then she looked up at Owen.

"I should have shared it with you, my sweet husband."

"Ah yes," Mr. Jones said. "Jude and I were right."

"Right?" Emalyn said and hugged tightly to Owen.

"But yes," Mr. Jones said. "We are treasure hunters. And didn't we have a perfect find in the two of you? True love is the greatest treasure of all. Come along, Jude, we've work to do."

"Isn't there one more surprise?" Jude said.

"Ah, certainly."

The angel Mr. Jones lifted his arms.

"Come," he said.

From beside him stepped four people.

"Mama? Papa?" Emalyn cried and rushed over to them. "Oh, I've missed you both so."

Owen ran and embraced his own mother and father.

"Emalyn gave me a portrait of you," he said. "I've longed to see you both again."

"Let's be off, Mr. Jones," Jude said. "We must check on Master Percy. Granted, you gave him to Fiona, but that boy needs special attention."

Mr. Jones looked back at Emalyn and nodded his head.

"Your treasures," he said and smiled.

The Treasures

Dungarran is a thriving town at the north edge of County Tipperary just beyond the Golden Vale. Fed by the River Shannon, its pastoral lands, green and verdant, sweep along the countryside in great swaths peopled by magnificent herds of cattle and black-faced sheep. Close to the nearby town of Clonmel, Dungarran neighbors the economic hub of the county.

People thrive there.

Twenty years after the second bombing, the Dunaghy-Meade Celtic High Cross still stands at the entrance to the busy town, a symbol of the both the sanctity of ancient ways and the sacred duty each resident feels to honor growth and remember those who came before them.

Aside from an enormous but abandoned castle atop a distant hill near the Galtee Mountains—a castle said to be haunted—Dunaghy Manor stands as an elegant tribute to the success of those who have lived there. Marked by a tall black gate emblazoned with a pair of swans, the manor is home to a woman named Fiona and her son, Percy, a minister in the local Anglican church. Though Fiona has no grandchildren, she contents herself with operating a large guest house designed for travelers or those who find themselves in need of a hot meal or a warm place to stay. Not even beggars are turned away.

That this small family has been blessed by God is apparent in their loving attitudes toward others, attitudes which did not always exist.

Young Percy, though he had a rough start, attributes his salvation to his dog, one Mr. Jones. For a short while after the two of them first met at Mr. Owen Meade's funeral, Mr. Jones disappeared, but Percy insists that his broken heart at losing the dog brought Mr. Jones running back to him in the middle of a cold and windy night. And though the dog must be nearing thirty years of age, he never seems to age and remains Percy's faithful companion.

His mother, Fiona—a gentle soul—inherited Dunaghy Manor from her beloved Emalyn. On the day of her husband Owen's funeral, Emalyn was found slumped beside the casket. At first, Fiona thought her girl was only sleeping. She had a sweet smile on her lovely face and seemed so very peaceful. But when not even Fiona could rouse the sleeping beauty, she knew that her sweet Emalyn had succumbed to her grief. She'd often heard her and Owen say that they were like swans. They mated for life and if one of them passed away, the other was sure to die of a broken heart.

To honor her two beloved "children," Fiona built an enormous pond in front of Dunaghy Manor, and in it she put two white swans, who still, to this day, glide across the water in perfect contentment. When baby swans began to appear, Fiona simply had the pond enlarged so that the whole of the swan family could reside there peaceably.

When tourists come through the town of Dungarran, many of them ask to see the Swan House.

It does not disappoint. The swans are friendly to all, and will sometimes swim in tandem to chosen guests and nuzzle them with their necks. Tales are told that the swans have healing powers, and those who are touched find themselves free of whatever malady brought them there.

Occasionally, there are tours through the Manor proper. Tourists gaze at the fine furnishings, the elegant marble throughout, the enormous crystal chandeliers, a lovely scalloped-back, green velvet chair that graces the foyer, and stunning portraits of the Dunaghy/ Meade families.

But what attracts them most is a large gilded frame with a name-plate that reads: *The Beggar Jude.*

Some understand and nod their heads. Others seem puzzled, for inside the frame is a feather, one shimmering white feather. Scripted in gold on fine parchment underneath the feather are these words: *Emalyn's Treasure.*

 About the
Author

Joy Ross Davis is of Irish descent and a
student of the lore and magic found in the hills
of Tennessee. After a twenty-five year career as a
college English professor, she traveled to Ireland
and worked as a writer and photographer, pub-
lishing numerous travel articles and photos for
an Irish travel agency. She has been a contrib-
uting feature writer for a local newspaper and
has published articles in Southern literary mag-
azines. She lives in Alabama with her son and
beloved dogs. She loves to speak at conferences,
book club meetings, and events to share her
connection with angels and the stories behind
her books.

CPSIA information can be obtained
at www.ICGtesting.com
Printed in the USA
BVOW08s1100110517
483837BV00001B/39/P